Spirit Bear and Children Make History

Based on a True Story

Written by Cindy Blackstock and Eddy Robinson

Illustrated by Amanda Strong

Edited by Jennifer King and Sarah Howden

© 2020 by First Nations Child & Family Caring Society of Canada (2nd edition. Revised illustrations)

Originally published in 2017 by First Nations Child & Family Caring Society of Canada, Ottawa, ON

First Nations Child & Family Caring Society of Canada
fncaringsociety.com | info@fncaringsociety.com | @Caringsociety

Art Direction and Illustration: Amanda Strong | spottedfawnproductions.com
Additional Illustration: Dora Cepic, Erin Banda and Natty Boonmasiri
Design and Layout: Leah Gryfe Designs | leahgryfedesigns.com
Edited by Jennifer King and Sarah Howden

Quoted text on pages 44–45 from Spirit Bear's Osgoode Hall honorary "Bearrister" degree.

Printed in Canada

To Jordan River Anderson, founder of Jordan's Principle, his loving family, and Norway House Cree Nation for the gift of Jordan's Principle. And to all First Nations children and other children who stand with them to implement the Truth and Reconciliation Commission's Calls to Action.

4

Bear Facts

Hello, friends! My name is Spirit Bear. Let me tell you about myself!

- I am a member of the Carrier Sekani Tribal Council in British Columbia
- My mom is Mary the Bear, and I have three sisters: Era Bear, Cedar Bear, and Memengwe Bear
- My name is Sus Zul in the Carrier language
- I am a "Bearrister." My job is to help kids like you stand up for the fair treatment of First Nations children
- My favourite foods are huckleberries and COOKIES!
- I love kids and hugs
- I was born on May 10, 2007

Did you know that the government of Canada is supposed to look after all the children who live here equally? The problem is, it doesn't. First Nations kids get less money than other children for things they need, like health care, education, help for their families, and basics such as clean water.

Canadian Human Rights Tribunal

So in February 2007, two First Nations groups (the First Nations Child and Family Caring Society—we call it the Caring Society for short—and the Assembly of First Nations) went to the Canadian Human Rights Tribunal to try to change that. A Tribunal is like a court where groups can go to try to solve a problem.

People from the First Nations and the government of Canada talked to the Tribunal members (who are like judges) to explain their sides of the story. The government of Canada tried to stop the Tribunal from hearing the case.

It took *six years* for the hearing to officially start, *almost two years* for the hearing itself, and then *over a year* for a decision to be made. That's *nine years*!

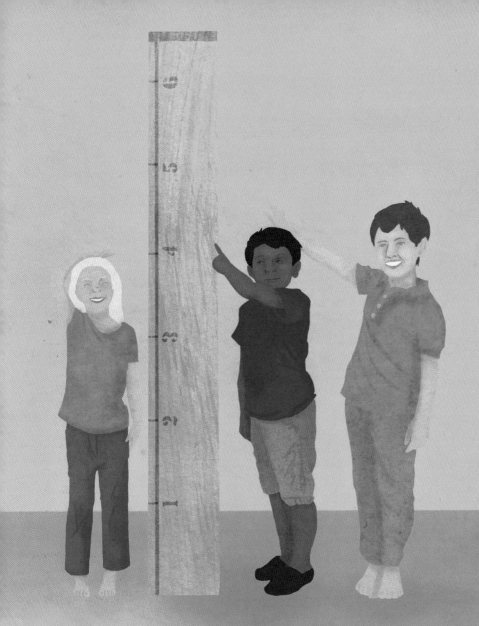

I was born on May 10, 2007, in the huckleberry patches in Carrier Sekani territory near Prince George, British Columbia. My mom, Mary the Bear, worked with the people at Carrier Sekani Family Services to help children and families be healthy and proud.

Mom taught me that when I see someone being treated badly, I need to find out what's happening and do what I can to help make things better.

11

So when my mom told me about the Tribunal, I took a very LONG trip from Carrier Sekani territory to Ottawa, Ontario, to go and watch, and to stand up for First Nations kids.

And I wasn't the only one! Lots of children came too—to listen, and to show they cared.

I believe that children can change the world because I saw it happen at the Tribunal. This is the story of how these kids—kids just like you—made a difference. And how bears like me, and other animals too, helped along the way!

October 2008

Here I am, in Canada's capital city! I learned that Ottawa is on the lands of the Algonquin First Nations peoples and the name of the city comes from the Algonquin word *adàwe*, which means "trade." I like Ottawa, but I miss my family. Hey, look! There is my very dear friend Cindy the Sheep.

Cindy lives on a farm near Kamloops, British Columbia, and she came to watch the hearings, along with some First Nations people from across Canada ... but where is everyone else? I wish more people would come to help!

14

A STATION

15

September 2009

As we sit together in the hearing room, Cindy tells me that First Nations groups took this complaint to the Tribunal so that First Nations children and families could get the help they need from child welfare services.

These services help keep kids safe, at home with their families, and connected to their culture.

18

Cindy also tells me about a very special boy named Jordan River Anderson from Norway House Cree Nation in Manitoba.

Jordan was born on October 22, 1999, in Winnipeg, Manitoba, with a serious health condition. Doctors said he

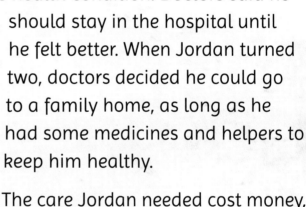

should stay in the hospital until he felt better. When Jordan turned two, doctors decided he could go to a family home, as long as he had some medicines and helpers to keep him healthy.

The care Jordan needed cost money, and the governments of Manitoba and Canada could not agree on which one should pay, because Jordan was a First Nations child.

They argued for so long that Jordan got sick again and passed away.

Named after Jordan, Jordan's Principle is a guiding rule saying that arguments about money should not stop kids from getting the help they need— like visits to doctors, or extra support in school—when they need it. It's what this Tribunal case is all about.

June 2010

A few years have gone by since I came to Ottawa, and the Tribunal is still going on. Only Cindy the Sheep and I are watching as the government tries to stop the Tribunal from hearing about the unfairness to First Nations kids ...

But when I look up, my hope comes to life! A group of high school students just walked in. I am so happy!

They've come to bear witness, which means to watch and listen and learn about what is going on so they can tell other people what is happening and let them know how they can help.

The students invite others to come too. Soon the Tribunal hearing room is full of young people of all ages, who give me lots of hugs and tell me what they are learning!

February 14, 2012

Now it's Valentine's Day, and the government is still trying to stop the Tribunal from taking on the case. Some kids are inside a big courthouse watching the hearing, while hundreds of others are outside on Parliament Hill reading the letters they wrote to the government of Canada for Have a Heart Day!

The children are asking the government to make sure First Nations kids have a fair chance to grow up safely with their families, get a good education, be healthy, and feel proud of who they are.

On days when the Tribunal is not happening, Cindy and I visit people across Canada to tell them how First Nations kids are not treated equally. When people learn about what's going on, they want to help! I give out lots of hugs to thank them.

February 2013

I have wonderful news! My sister Era Bear has come to live with me!

Era tells me that learning about the unfair way Indigenous peoples have been treated and helping to fix it is called "reconciliation."

On her way to Ottawa, Era heard Indigenous grown-ups share sad stories about the way they were treated as children with a group called the Truth and Reconciliation Commission (TRC).

33

The TRC has lots of Calls to Action to help us learn from the past and do all we can to honour and respect Indigenous peoples' rights, cultures, and languages. Did you know there are over fifty Indigenous languages in Canada? That is a lot of ways to say Spirit Bear!

35

February 25, 2013

After years of the government trying to shut down the case, the Tribunal has agreed that it can officially go ahead starting today!

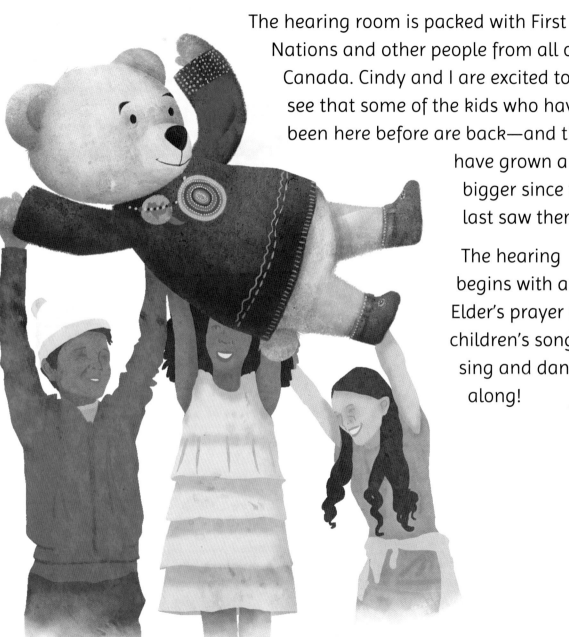

The hearing room is packed with First Nations and other people from all over Canada. Cindy and I are excited to see that some of the kids who have been here before are back—and they have grown a lot bigger since we last saw them!

The hearing begins with an Elder's prayer and children's songs. I sing and dance along!

October 24, 2014

The Tribunal hearings are finally over! Now we have to
wait for the decision.

I don't like waiting—I get butterflies in my stomach—but the good memories of the children who held me, told me their stories, and dressed me up make me feel better. Plus, now I have more clothes than Cindy the Sheep (and she LOVES fashion)!

January 26, 2016 — The Decision!

I am *beary* happy!!!

After nine years, the Tribunal said the government was discriminating (giving First Nations kids less because they are First Nations) and ruled that First Nations children must get proper funding for the help they need!

Children are cheering and saying they will keep working until the change actually happens.

May 10, 2016

It's my ninth birthday, or *bearthday* in the bear world! Cindy and I are celebrating with other children and grown-ups who bring their bears to daycare, school, and work to spread the word about Jordan's Principle. We call it Bear Witness Day!

EQUITY 4 First Nations

43

August 1, 2016

Cindy and I are at Norway House Cree Nation, where Jordan's family lives, for the Jordan's Principle Parade!

Every year, children gather their teddies to march in a parade to celebrate Jordan's Principle! Stuffies like me were Jordan's favourite toys.

June 23, 2017

Wow! After ten long years of learning about the mistreatment of First Nations kids and doing what I could to help, I am getting an honorary "Bearrister" degree from Osgoode Hall Law School for my "courageous support and bearing witness throughout a long and difficult process of truth-telling and healing."

My mom says everyone at the Carrier Sekani Tribal Council is very proud of me, and they hope all children and bear cubs work hard at school and help with reconciliation.

Just because we're small doesn't mean we can't stand tall

48

I am super proud of all the children who stood up for fairness at the Tribunal. By being there and by writing their letters for Have a Heart Day, they gave strength to the cause. They were saying: we want the unfairness to stop.

Don't forget: "Just because you're small doesn't mean you can't stand tall!" After all, no one would think a bear could be a "Bearrister," but here I am!

The government is starting to listen and things are getting better ... but many First Nations children still don't get things other kids have, like safe and comfy schools and clean drinking water.

Let's join hands—and paws and hooves—and keep working together until *every* First Nations child is treated fairly!

Remember: *Every child matters!* *You matter!*

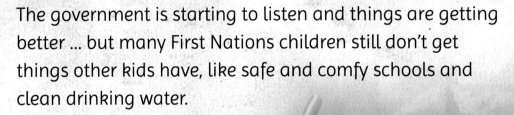

EVERY CHILD
MATTERS

Timeline

October 22, 1999
Jordan River Anderson's
birthday

February 2, 2005
Jordan River Anderson
passes away

February 23, 2007
Human rights complaint
filed by Caring Society
and Assembly of
First Nations

May 10, 2007
Spirit Bear's birthday

October 2008
Spirit Bear
goes to Ottawa

September 2009
Hearings begin but are
quickly met with delays

June 2010
Students come
to bear witness

February 14, 2012
First annual
Have a Heart Day

February 2013
Era Bear comes to
live with Spirit Bear, and
the case officially begins
at the Tribunal

October 24, 2014
End of the Tribunal
hearings

January 26, 2016
The kids win! Tribunal
releases its decision

May 10, 2016
Spirit Bear's ninth
bearthday and the first
Bear Witness Day

August 1, 2016
Jordan's Principle
Parade in Norway House
Cree Nation

June 23, 2017
Spirit Bear gets an
honorary "Bearrister"
degree from Osgoode
Hall Law School

October 20, 2017
Indigenous Bar
Association admits
Spirit Bear to the "Bear"

Find learning resources and fun and free ways you can
help at: **www.fncaringsociety.com**

Meet Spirit Bear and Cindy the Sheep

Spirit Bear: A member of the Carrier Sekani Tribal Council, Spirit Bear represents the 165,000 First Nations children impacted by the First Nations child welfare case at the Canadian Human Rights Tribunal, as well as the thousands of other children who have committed to learning about the case and have taken part in peaceful and respectful actions in support of reconciliation and equity. Spirit Bear has a "Bearrister" degree from Osgoode Hall Law School and in October 2017 was admitted to the "Bear" by the Indigenous Bar Association.

Cindy the Sheep: The real Cindy the Sheep lives on a farm in British Columbia and is the proud winner of several agricultural awards. Her mom's name is Wish and her sister's name is Lou. Cindy loves snacks—especially whole oats, grain, hay, and fries from the fair! She is also known for her keen sense of fashion.